W9-DBB-957

LIONEL
◆ AND ◆
HIS FRIENDS

LIONEL
◆ AND ◆
HIS FRIENDS

by Stephen Krensky
pictures by Susanna Natti

Dial Books for Young Readers   *New York*

For all the friends on Eaton Road
S.K.

For Michael Willsky
S.N.

Published by Dial Books for Young Readers
A Division of Penguin Books USA Inc.
375 Hudson Street
New York, New York 10014

First Edition
1 3 5 7 9 10 8 6 4 2
Library of Congress Cataloging in Publication Data
Krensky, Stephen.
Lionel and his friends / by Stephen Krensky;
pictures by Susanna Natti.
p. cm.
Summary: Lionel and his friends have dinner, trade sandwiches
at school, eavesdrop on Louise and Emily, and play baseball.
ISBN 0-8037-1750-4 (trade). — ISBN 0-8037-1751-2 (library)
[1. Friendship—Fiction.] I. Natti, Susanna, ill. II.Title.
PZ7.K883Lh 1996 [Fic]—dc20 94-37434 CIP AC

Reading Level 1.9

The full-color artwork was prepared using pencil,
colored pencils, and watercolor washes.

CONTENTS

THE IMPOSTOR

Lionel and his friend Max

were playing together at Lionel's house.

They went to the kitchen for a snack.

Lionel's mother was there,

putting away some groceries.

"Do you need any help?" Max asked.

"Thank you, Max," she said.

She looked at Lionel.

"You can help too," she said.

Lionel frowned.

As they were finishing,
Louise came home
wearing new sneakers.
"What do you think?"
she asked her mother.
"Perfect," said Mother.

"I like them too," said Max.

"You do?" said Louise.

She looked at Lionel.

"You could learn a few things

from your friends," she said.

Lionel frowned again.

At dinner Lionel's father asked Max

if he wanted more squash.

"Thanks," said Max.

"It's delicious."

Lionel frowned his biggest frown yet.

After dinner

Lionel pulled Max into his room.

"All right," he said, "what's going on?"

"What do you mean?" Max asked.

Lionel folded his arms.

"The real Max isn't so polite
and helpful," he said.

"He doesn't like new sneakers.
And he hates squash."

Lionel looked hard at Max.

"You're not the real Max.
You must be an impostor."

Max laughed.

"I am too the real Max," he said. "Honest."

Lionel was not convinced.

"Who got in trouble last week for flying paper airplanes in class?"

"Jeffrey," said Max.

"True," Lionel admitted.

"Now tell me Polly's middle name."

Max sighed.

"She doesn't have one," he said.

Lionel sighed.

"I guess you're the real Max,"

he said.

"Why are you acting so strange?"

"I don't know," said Max.

"But you acted the same way
at my house yesterday."

"I did?" said Lionel.

Max nodded.

"You offered to help my father

clean the basement," he said.

"And later you told my sister

how good her homework looked."

Lionel turned red.

"You're right."

"Maybe it's a disease,"
said Max.
"The kind you only catch
at other people's houses."

"Maybe," said Lionel.

"If it is, let's hope

we both get better soon."

THE SANDWICH

Lionel sat down

in the school cafeteria.

Everyone else started eating lunch.

Lionel just took out his sandwich

and put it on the table.

He stared at it.

"What's the matter, Lionel?"

asked Susie. "Why aren't you eating?"

Lionel sighed.

"My father made the wrong thing today," he said.

Jeffrey took a look.

"It's peanut butter and jelly," he said.

"That's what you always have."

Lionel shook his head.

"This is jelly and peanut butter,"

he said.

"My father made it wrong."

"He put the jelly on first."

Ellen nodded.

"Sometimes my mother
makes me chocolate milk.
She puts the milk in the glass
before the powder

instead of the other way around.

It never tastes the same."

"Why didn't your father make you

another sandwich?" Jeffrey asked.

Lionel frowned.

"He said there wasn't time."

"Maybe you could turn it over,"
said Susie.

Lionel shook his head.

"That wouldn't help," he said.

"Then it would just be
jelly and peanut butter upside down."

"You know, Lionel," said Neil,

"I like jelly and peanut butter

sandwiches.

Do you want to trade?"

Lionel's face brightened.

"What do you have instead?" he asked.

"Tuna fish," said Neil.

"Solid white?" Lionel asked.

Neil nodded.

"Cut in half sideways, not triangles?"

Neil nodded again.

"White bread?"

Neil nodded some more.

"Okay," said Lionel.

They made the trade.

Lionel inspected his new sandwich.

"By the way," he said,

"what kind of mayonnaise is this?"

"Regular," said Neil.

Good thing, thought Lionel,

as he happily took a bite.

THE MEETING

Lionel and Jeffrey were
crawling through the grass.
"Quiet," whispered Lionel.
"We're getting close.
And aliens have big ears."
Jeffrey lowered his head.
"Do you think they're dangerous?"
he asked.
Lionel thought so.

"After spending all that time in space," he said, "they're bound to be cranky. Especially the ugly one with the yellow hair." They crept a little closer.

The alien with the yellow hair
was speaking.

"The time has come," said Louise.

"Are you sure?" said Emily.

"I'm sure," said Louise.

"I'm going to get rid of *him*
once and for all.
When I'm done,
there won't be a trace of *him* left."
Lionel and Jeffrey looked at each other.

What were these aliens plotting?

And who was this mysterious *him*

they were talking about?

They wriggled forward to hear more.

"How are you going to do it?"

asked Megan.

"I'm not sure," said Louise.

"There are so many possibilities."

"What about tying *him* to a rocket,"

said Emily,

"and blasting him into space?"

"Too uncertain," said Louise.

"He might come back,

like a comet or something."

"What about boiling *him* in oil?"

"Too messy," said Louise.

"I'd have to clean the pot afterward."

"Maybe quicksand," said Megan.

"Maybe," said Louise.

"It certainly would be neat."

"Won't your parents get suspicious?"

wondered Emily.

Louise shook her head.

"They'll believe whatever I tell them.

With Lionel anything's possible."

Lionel and Jeffrey shared

a horrified glance.

Lionel was the *him* they were discussing.

"Of course," said Emily,

"you still need to get your hands

on *him*."

Louise stood up to stretch.

"Oh, that won't be too hard. . . . "

She jumped over to where the boys
were hiding.

"WILL IT, LIONEL?"

Both boys jumped up.

"Run!" cried Lionel.

"Run for your life!" said Jeffrey.

The three girls watched them go.

Then they started laughing.

"Did you see their faces?" said Emily.

"They'll think twice before sneaking up on us again," said Megan.

Louise sighed.

"At least for today," she said.

PLAY BALL

Lionel and his friends
were playing baseball.
Lionel was getting a lot of advice.
"Dive for those balls, Lionel,"
said Jeffrey, when a ball got past him.
"Catch with two hands," said Sarah,
when a ball jumped off his glove.
When Lionel came up to bat,
Ellen was pitching.
"Easy out," she said.

Lionel gripped the bat firmly.

He would show her how wrong she was.

Ellen made her windup.

The pitch sailed in.

Lionel waited—and then he swung hard.

The bat met the ball

with a sharp *Craaccck!*

The ball went up and up and up.

It sailed over a fence.

CRASH!

"That sounded like a window,"

said Max.

"At the Barries'," said Sarah.

Lionel froze.

He squeezed his eyes shut.

This was going to be terrible.

Mr. Barrie was bound to yell at him.

His parents would find out.

They would yell too.

Lionel opened his eyes.

Mr. Barrie was approaching

with a ball in his hand.

"Who hit this ball?" he asked.

Lionel swallowed hard.

He didn't want anyone else

getting in trouble for his mistake.

"I did," he said.

"I hit it too," said Jeffrey behind him.

He had picked up his bat.

"And me," said Max,

his bat now resting on his shoulder.

"I got a piece of it," said George.

"Don't forget me," said Sarah.

"And us," said everyone else together.

They were all holding their bats.

Mr. Barrie looked around.

"I see," he said, trying to look serious.

"It was a real team effort."

He rubbed his chin.

"Well, since you all shared in the hit,

you can all help me fix

the window later.

Fair enough?"

Everyone nodded.

Mr. Barrie returned to his house.

Lionel looked at everybody and sighed.

"Thanks," he said.

Jeffrey smiled.

"It could have been any of us.

Besides," he added,

"that's what friends are for."

O dainty duck, O dear!

William Shakespeare, *A Midsummer Night's Dream*

Wild ducks always do that. Dive down to the bottom as
deep as they can go, and hold on with their beaks to
the seaweed...and they never come up again.

Henrik Ibsen, *The Wild Duck*

There's no more valour in that Poins
than in a wild duck.

William Shakespeare, *Henry IV, Part I*

A garden saw I, ful of blosmy bowes,
Upon a river, in a grene mede,
There as that swetnesse evermore y-now is,
With floures whyte, blewe, yelowe, and rede;
And cold well-stremes, no-thing dede,
That swommen ful of smale fisshes lighte,
With finnes red and scales silver-brighte.
The Parlement of foules.

Geoffrey Chaucer, 'The Parlement of Foules'

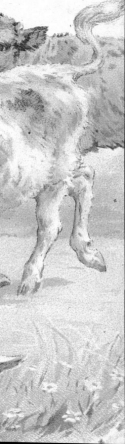

Jemima Puddle-Duck was a simpleton: no[t even] the
mention of sage and onions made her susp[icious. She]
went round the farm-garden, nibbling off sm[all samples of]
the different sorts of herbs that are used f[or stuffing]
roast duck.

Beatrix Potter, *The Tale of Jemima Puddle-D[uck]*

The great egg burst at last. 'Tchick: tchick[!' said the]
little one, and out it tumbled – but, oh! ho[w big and]
ugly it was. The Duck looked at i[t, and said,]
'That is a great, strong creature,' said she; '[and none of the]
others are at all like it.'

Hans Andersen, 'The Ugly Duckling'

Enjoy the Spring of Love and You[th,]
To some good angel leave the res[t;]
For Time will teach thee soon the tr[uth,]
There are no birds in last year's ne[st.]

Henry Wadsworth Longfellow

All along the backwater,
Through the rushes tall,
Ducks are a-dabbling.
Up tails all!

Ducks' tails, drakes' tails,
Yellow feet a-quiver,
Yellow bills all out of sight
Busy in the river!

Slushy green undergrowth
Where the roach swim —
Here we keep our larder,
Cool and full and dim.

Every one for what he likes!
We like to be
Heads down, tails up,
Dabbling free!

High in the blue above
Swifts whirl and call —
We are down a-dabbling
Up tails all!

Kenneth Grahame, 'Ducks' Ditty'

Whatever ducklings see when they hatch
becomes 'mother' as far as they are concerned,
even it happens to be a human being, a dog, or
an orange balloon. Just so long as it is a large
moving object, they will accept it as the 'parent to
be followed'.

Desmond Morris, *Animal Watching*

The long light shakes across the lake,
The forces of the morning quake,
The dawn is slant across the lawn,
Here is no eft or mortal snake
But only sluggish duck and drake....

T. S. Eliot, 'Lines to a Duck in the Park'

Douglas Hall

Charley Barley, butter and eggs,
Sold his wife for three duck eggs.
When the ducks began to lay
Charley Barley flew away.

English nursery rhyme

The duck, 'anas' in Latin, gets its name from its love of
swimming (natandi). Some kinds of duck are called
German, and these fatten better than the rest. The
goose gets its name from the duck ('anser', from 'anas')
either because they are similar or because they both
love swimming. All species of birds are born twice. For
first the egg is born, and then the chick or duckling is
formed by the warmth of the mother's body and given
life. They are called eggs because they are full of
moisture. Things that have moisture on the outside are
simply damp, but if they have moisture within, they
carry life in them.

An English Bestiary, MS AD 764, Bodleian Library, Oxford

To a man, ornithologists are tall, slender, and
bearded so that they can stand motionless for
hours, imitating kindly trees,
as they watch for birds.

Gore Vidal

From Peticote I put up a pair of Red-legged
Partridge, and from the marsh first a pair and
then a wisp of twelve Snipe. I also surprised a
couple of what I took to be Mallard, but as the
drake flew past I glimpsed a white patch on his
breast and wondered...he had the typical
bottle-green head and neck, curly tail feathers
and grey and brown upper parts, but the neck-
ring was replaced by that large, uneven breast
patch, the speculum was green instead of
purple, and the flanks and belly were a rich,
dark chestnut. I wondered if he could be a
Mallard Shoveler hybrid.

Benjamin Perkins, *A Year in the Meadow*

Spring rain:
The uneaten ducks
Quack.

Haiku by Kobayashi Issa

Dull day,
dark day,
definitely a
duck day!
Anonymous

Among the notes of the
numerous birds, I
recognized those of the
thrush, blackbird, hedge
sparrow, sky-lark, wren,
great tit, chaffinch, green-
finch, red wagtail, yellow
bunting and under cover of
the rushes, a duck or two.

A Country Woman's Diary

Happier of happy though I be, like them
I cannot take possession of the sky,
Mount with a thoughtless impulse, and wheel there,
One of a mighty multitude whose way
And motion is a harmony and dance
Magnificent.

William Wordsworth, 'Home at Grasmere'

Like water off a duck's back.

Proverb

When you have shot one bird flying you have shot all
birds flying. They are all different and they fly in
different ways but the sensation is the same and the
last one is as good as the first.

Ernest Hemingway

When you are tired of life, turn to ducks.

Anonymous

Ducks require no ship and sail
Bellied on the foamy skies,
Who scud north.

John Crowe Ransom, 'What Ducks Require'

The horses, the cows, the calves, the sheep, the farm dogs, the ducks and the hens — are all very well thank you; except a brown duck called Tapioca, who has rheumatism; and a hen with a sore toe who had a cow tread on her foot, and I have her in a basket until it is better.

Beatrix Potter, Letter to Dulcie, 29 December 1924

Put a duck on a lake in the midst of some swans, and you'll discover he'll miss his pond and eventually return to it.

Emile Augier

Prisoner, God has given you good abilities, instead of which you go about the country stealing ducks.

William Arabin, *Arabinesque at Law*

By shallow rivers, to whose falls, Melodious birds sing madrigals.

Christopher Marlowe

The imperial Consort of the Fairy-king
Owns not a sylvan bower; or gorgeous cell
With emerald floored, and with purpureal shell
Ceilinged and roofed; that is so fair a thing
As this low structure, for the tasks of Spring,
Prepared by one who loves the buoyant swell
Of the brisk waves, yet here consents to dwell;
And spreads its steadfast peace her brooding wing.
Words cannot paint the o'ershadowing yew-tree bough,
And dimly-gleaming Nest, – a hollow crown
Of golden leaves inlaid with silver down,
Fine as the mother's softest plumes allow;
I gazed – and, self-accused while gazing, sighed
For human-kind, weak slaves of cumbrous pride!

William Wordsworth, 'The Wild Duck's Nest'

The duck and the drake,
Shall watch at this wake.

John Skelton, 'Requiem Mass for Philip Sparrow'

Behold the duck.
It does not cluck.
A cluck it lacks.
It quacks.
It is especially fond
Of a puddle or a pond.
When it dines or sups,
It bottoms ups.

Ogden Nash, 'The Duck'

She shall get a duke, my dear,
As ducks do get a drake....

Anonymous, 'A Dis A Dis, A Green Grass'

Office against Katharine Thompson and Anne
Nevelson, pretended to be common charmers of sick
folkes...that they use to bring white ducks or drakes,
and to sett the bill thereof to the mouth of the sick
person, and mumble upp their charmes in such a
strange manner as is damnible and horrible.

Depositions, York Castle, 23 July 1604

There is a passion for hunting something deeply
implanted in the human breast.

Charles Dickens, *Oliver Twist*

Four ducks on a pond,
A grass bank beyond,
A blue sky of spring,
White clouds on the wing;
What a little thing
To remember for years –
To remember with tears.

William Allingham, 'Four Ducks on a Pond'

You'll float as merrily, I undertake,
As any lily-white duck behind her drake.

Geoffrey Chaucer, *The Miller's Tale*

All Nature seems at work. Slugs leave their lair –
The bees are stirring – birds are on the wing –
And Winter slumbering in the open air,
Wears on his smiling face a dream of Spring!
And I the while, the sole unbusy thing,
Nor honey make, nor pair, nor build, nor sing.

Samuel Taylor Coleridge, 'Work Without Hope'

...at midday, he would pause and eat the pasty that his
wife had baked for him, and sitting on the cliff's edge
would watch the birds. Autumn was best for this, better
than spring. In spring the birds flew inland, purposeful,
intent; they knew where they were bound, the rhythm
and ritual of their life brooked no delay. In autumn,
those that had not migrated overseas, but remained to
pass the winter were caught up in the same driving
urge, but because migration was denied them followed
a pattern of their own.

Daphne du Maurier, *The Birds*

'I've seen it all,
Down the pond's bottom,' –
The look on the duckling's face.

Haiku by Naito Joso

I tore your letter into strips
No bigger than the airy feathers
That ducks preen out in changing weathers
Upon the shifting ripple-tips.

Thomas Hardy, 'The Torn Letter'

Duck: wild and domestic waterfowl of the family
Anatidae. It is hunted and bred for its meat, eggs, and
feathers. A duck is the female of the species; the male
is a drake. Ducks have waterproof feathers, with a
thick layer of down underneath, and webbed feet.
They are usually divided into three groups: surface-
feeding – such as the mallard, wood duck and teal,
which frequent ponds and quiet waters; diving – such
as the canvasback and eider, found on bays,
rivers and lakes; and fish-eating, or mergansers,
which also prefer open water.

Dictionary definition

Why do ducks fly south in winter?
Because it's too far to walk.

Anonymous

The sea dark,
The call of the teal
Dimly white.

Haiku by Matsuo Basho

Over the mountain ledge
Flights of wild duck
Noisily go;
But I am lonely,
For you are not here.

Empress Saimei, *From the Age of the Gods*

From troubles of the world
I turn to ducks
Beautiful comical things.

F. W. Harvey, *Ducks and Other Verses*

Like a flight of wild duck
We, her servants, bobbed in the water,
Thronging to gather the beams
And carry them to the streams of Izumi.

Hitomaro, *The Construction of the Palace of Fujiwara*

Even the wild duck
Sleep close by their mates,
Lest on their tails
The hoar-frost fall.

Tajihi, 'Lamenting His Wife's Death'

I was wondering where the ducks went when the
lagoon got all icy and frozen over. I wondered if some
guy came in a truck and took them away to a zoo or
something. Or if they just flew away.

J. D. Salinger, *The Catcher in the Rye*

Ah, sweet ducks!

Shakespeare, *Troilus and Cressida*

Twilight, red in the west.
Dimness, a glow on the wood.
The teams plod home to rest.
The wild duck comes to glean.
Oh should not understood,
What thinks have the farm ducks seen
They cry so — huddle and cry?
Only the soul that goes.
Eager. Eager. Flying.
Over the globe of the moon,
Over the wood that glows.
Wings liked. Necks a-strain,
A rush and a wild crying.
A cry of pain
In the reds of a steel lagoon,
In a land that no man knows.

John Masefield, 'The Wild Duck'

I can swim like a duck, I'll be sworn.

William Shakespeare, *The Tempest*

Duck Variations

Title of play by David Mamet

If ducks flied at Hallowtide (31 October), at Christmastide the ducks will swim. If ducks swim at Hallowtide, at Christmastide the ducks will slide.

Traditional

'Ha! Ha!', said the Duck, laughing.

Rudyard Kipling, *The Day's Work*

Antony claps on his sea-wing, and like a doting mallard
Leaving the fight in height, flies after her.

William Shakespeare, *Antony and Cleopatra*

But first I must tell you I heard a noise just now like
somebody talking in the kitchen – there was Mr Drake
Puddleduck and six Mrs Ducks sitting on the mat
before the kitchen fire!! Our servant had gone out and
left the back door open and it was raining very hard.
But that is no excuse for ducks, they like rain. Had it
been hens, or turkeys, I should not have been
surprised. I said 'Whatever are you doing here Mr
Puddleduck?' And off they waddled in a hurry, Mrs
Possy-Duck always last; she is quite blind of one eye.
She runs against apple trees, etc., but she seems as fat
as any so I suppose she can find worms and corn to eat.

Beatrix Potter, Letter to June Steele, 8 May 1933

They are not those who used to feed us
When we were young – they cannot be –
These shapes that now bereave and bleed us?
They are not those who used to feed us,
For did we then cry, they would heed us.
      – If hearts can house such treachery
They are not those who used to feed us
When we were young – they cannot be!

Thomas Hardy, 'The Puzzled Game Birds'

Among the tawny tasselled reed
The ducks and ducklings float and feed
With head oft dabbing in the flood
They fish all day the weedy mud
And tumbler-like are bobbing there,
      Heels topsy-turvy in the air,
Then up and quack and down they go,
      Heel over head again below.

John Clare, 'The Fens'

In some species of ducks...certain specific kinds of displacement activities have become so closely linked to particular courtship situations that they have become incorporated into specially evolved displays. The drakes employ highly modified preening actions that bring into prominence brightly coloured patches of feathers. The preening has become no more than a single swipe at the feathers, with the bill being aimed at the display patch. In the mandarin, the displacement preening movement has become the touching of a large display feather; in the garganey, the bill is moved to the outside of the bright blue wing-coverts, drawing special attention to them. In the mallard, the evolution of the displacement preening action has taken a different direction. There it has become a sound signal, the drake dragging the tip of his bill across the base of the large pinion quills. This makes a loud rrrrr sound, easily audible to the courted female.

Desmond Morris, *Animal Watching*

It is very strange, and very melancholy,
that the paucity of human pleasures
should persuade us ever to call hunting
one of them.

Samuel Johnson

'I'm keepin' secrets all th' time,' he said. 'If
I couldn't keep secrets from th'other lads,
secrets about foxes' cubs, an' birds' nests,
an' wild things' holes, there'd be naught
safe on th' moor. Aye, I can keep secrets.'

Frances Hodgson Burnett, *The Secret Garden*

The ten hours' light is abating,
And a late bird wings across,
Where the pines, like waltzers waiting
Give their black heads a toss.

Thomas Hardy, 'At Day-Close in November'

A duck...was brought to the little patient's side and the
bird's head was thrust into the child's open mouth, and
held there for about five...minutes, for nine successive
mornings. By that time the inflammation [of the mouth]
had disappeared.

N & Q, 1881

With his apology
For wings, as best he can
The duck flies.

Anonymous, *Senryu*

NOTES ON ILLUSTRATIONS

Page 6 *Puddle Ducks* by Douglas Hall; **Page 11** *Feeding Ducks*, illustration from "Where Lilies Live" by Edith Berkeley, c.1889. Courtesy of the Bridgeman Art Library; **Pages 12-13** *An Anxious Moment* by Briton Riviere (Royal Holloway & Bedford New College, Surrey). Courtesy of the Bridgeman Art Library; **Page 15** *Deck Duck* by Douglas Hall; **Page 17** *Ducks and Ducklings by a Pond* by John Frederick Herring Snr (Christie's, London). Courtesy of the Bridgeman Art Library; **Page 18** *Dear Little Ducks*, courtesy of the Laurel Clark Collection; **Page 20** *Duck on the Eighth* by Douglas Hall; **Pages 22-3** *Ducks on a Pond* by Alexander Koester (Josef Mensing Gallery). Courtesy of the Bridgeman Art Library; **Page 25** *Duck and Drake*, courtesy of the Laurel Clark Collection; **Page 26** *Ducks on the River Bank* by Carl Jutz (Christie's, London). Courtesy of the Bridgeman Art Library; **Page 28** *Juggle Duck* by Douglas Hall; **Page 30** *Duck and Ducklings*, courtesy of the Laurel Clark Collection; **Page 33** *Ducks in a Landscape* by David Adolph Constant Artz (Gavin Graham Gallery, London). Courtesy of the Bridgeman Art Library; **Page 36** *Classical Duck* by Douglas Hall; **Page 38** *An Urban Council* (panel) by Herbert William Weekes (Bonhams, London). Courtesy of the Bridgeman Art Library; **Pages 40-1** *Ducklings by the River's Edge* by David Adolph Constant Artz (Gavin Graham Gallery, London). Courtesy of the Bridgeman Art Library; **Page 42** *Ducks on Parade* by Douglas Hall; **Pages 44-5** *Dobbin and Ducks* Courtesy of the Laurel Clark Collection; **Page 47** *Little Ducks*. Courtesy of the Laurel Clark Collection. **Page 48** *Mother Duck with Ducklings in the Water* by David Adolph Constant Artz (Gavin Graham Gallery, London). Courtesy of the Bridgeman Art Library. **Page 51** *Pair Dancing on the River Bank* by Douglas Hall. **Page 52** *Come Pretty Swan and Ducklings Dear*, courtesy of the Laurel Clark Collection. **Page 54-5** *Mother with Ducks* by David Adolph Constant Artz (Gavin Graham Gallery, London). Courtesy of the Bridgeman Art Library. **Page 56** *Who's Afraid*. Courtesy of the Laurel Clark Collection. **Page 59** *Moonlight Duck* by Douglas Hall.

Acknowledgements: The Publishers wish to thank everyone who gave permission to reproduce the quotes in this book. Every effort has been made to contact the copyright holders, but in the event that an oversight has occurred, the publishers would be delighted to rectify any omissions in future editions of this book. Thomas Hardy reprinted courtesy of Penguin Books; *Good News Study Bible*, published by Thomas Nelson, 1986, extracts reprinted with their kind permission; *Penguin Book of Japanese Verse*, translated by Geoffrey Bownas and Anthony Thwaite, published by Penguin 1964, and reprinted with their permission; Ogden Nash, from *Verses from 1929*, reprinted by permission of Curtis Brown, Ltd. Copyright © 1942 by Ogden Nash, renewed; *The Tale of Jemima Puddleduck*, Beatrix Potter, reprinted courtesy of Frederick Warne and Co., a division of Penguin Book © Frederick Warne, renewed; Carmen Bernos de Gasztold, from *Prayers from the Ark*, translated by Rumer Godden, reprinted courtesy of Macmillan Publishing Company Ltd; Beatrix Potter's letters from *Letters to Children from Beatrix Potter*, collected and introduced by Judy Taylor, reprinted courtesy of Frederick Warne.and Co., a division of the Penguin Group; Kenneth Grahame, *The Wind in the Willows*, reprinted courtesy of Methuen Children's Books, text copyright The University Chest, Oxford, under the Berne Convention, copyright renewed; Daphne Du Maurier, *The Birds*, first published in a collection of short stories with the title, *The Apple Tree*, 1952, by Victor Gollancz, copyright © The Estate of Daphne du Maurier Browning, 1952; Katherine Mansfield, reprinted courtesy of Orion Books Limited; J. D. Salinger, reprinted courtesy of Penguin Books; *An English Bestiary* from the Bodleian Library, Oxford, MS Bodley 764.